C0-AAS-227

PAW PATROL

JUNGLE PUPS

Adapted by Frank Berrios
Based on the teleplay "Jungle Pups Save the Big, Big Animals" by Louise Moon
Illustrated by Nate Lovett

A Random House PICTUREBACK® Book

Random House 🏠 New York

© 2024 Spin Master Ltd. PAW PATROL and all related titles, logos, characters; and SPIN MASTER logo are trademarks of Spin Master Ltd. Used under license. Nickelodeon and all related titles and logos are trademarks of Viacom International Inc. Published in the United States by Random House Children's Books, a division of Penguin Random House LLC, 1745 Broadway, New York, NY 10019, and in Canada by Penguin Random House Canada Limited, Toronto. Pictureback, Random House, and the Random House colophon are registered trademarks of Penguin Random House LLC.
rhcbooks.com
ISBN 978-0-593-70955-9 (trade)
Printed in the United States of America
10 9 8 7 6 5 4 3 2 1

Early one morning, Ryder and the PAW Patrol pups were busy gathering treats for their jungle friends.

"The Hidden Jungle is such a magical place!" said Ryder.

"I can't wait to learn more about it!" replied Carlos. "I'm heading to the cave to study the old drawings in there."

When the pups went to look for their animal friends, the animals were nowhere to be found!

"There you are!" said Marshall, after finally spotting some elephants. "Are you all hiding from something?"

Suddenly, Marshall tripped and fell into what he thought was a huge hole. But then he realized something.

"Whoa! This is a really big paw print," he said. "No wonder the elephants are afraid!"

Marshall told Ryder about the scared animals and the big paw print.

"Don't worry," said Ryder. "We'll find out what's frightening them and what made the paw print. No paw print is too big, no pup is too small!" he added. "Jungle Pups to the Paw Patroller!"

Ryder gave the pups their assignments.

"Skye!" he said. "Fly over the jungle to see if you can find whatever made that paw print. Marshall! Talk to the animals and find out why they're so scared. Chase! Use your detective skills to investigate the print. Jungle pups are on the roll!"

Ryder and the pups went to see the paw print.
"Achoo!" sneezed Chase. "Some kind of cat must have made this.
It looks like a tiger print, but I've never seen one this big."

Marshall spotted something nearby.

"Nice gigantic kitty-cat!" he said. "I'm Marshall. What's your name?"

The saber-toothed tiger snarled . . . and then roared!

Thankfully, Marshall's elephant friends raced to the rescue!

"Strange," said Marshall. "That big tiger was limping. I wonder if it's hurt."

Just then, Ryder and Chase arrived. "Marshall? We heard a growl. Are you okay?"

Marshall told them about the huge cat with long, curved fangs.

"That sounds like a saber-toothed tiger!" said Ryder.

Ryder called Carlos, who told him that big cats had once lived in the area.

"How could an ancient cat be running around the jungle now?" asked Ryder.

"*No se.* I don't know," replied Carlos. "The Hidden Jungle is full of mysteries."

"This is one mystery we need to solve," said Chase. "Ryder to Jungle Pups. Be on the lookout for a saber-toothed tiger. We need to keep it away from other animals and find out how it got here."

Marshall and the elephants headed into the jungle, where they soon spotted a cloud that seemed to be coming out of the ground. "That's a weird-looking cloud," said Marshall—and then he and a young elephant slipped down an icy cliff!

"What happened to all the trees? *Brrr!* It's chilly down here!" said Marshall, after they had safely landed in the valley. Ryder and the pups quickly found the edge of the cliff.

"I see the valley!" said Skye from the air. "It doesn't look like the rest of the jungle, though. It's all frozen!"

Marshall wandered off on his own. A few rays of sunlight peeked through the clouds and landed on some ice chunks. Suddenly, the ice began to melt, revealing real, live woolly mammoths!

"Uh-oh, those shaggy ice elephants look thirsty and hungry," said Marshall. "Run!"

He and the animals started to run.

"Ryder, I think I found the place where the saber-toothed tiger came from—along with some other animals that have just thawed out!" Marshall yelled into his Pup Tag.

"Maybe a long time ago, the whole Hidden Jungle was hit by a sudden ice storm!" said Ryder. "Then most of the jungle warmed up later, but this valley stayed frozen until now."

"And the saber-toothed tiger must have thawed first," said Chase. "Now the others are thawing, too!"

Tracker used the cables on his monkey jeep to reach Marshall. Suddenly, a huge ape appeared! Tracker and his monkey friends tossed bananas to the ape.

"I never met a monkey who didn't like bananas. Even a giant one!" chuckled Tracker.

An ice storm started before the pups and their friend could find a way out of the valley. Then Marshall spotted the limping saber-toothed tiger again.

"Do you have a sore paw, kitty? Maybe I can help," he said.

Ryder called the pups on his Pup Pad. "PAW Patrol, can I get an update?"

"The storm is getting stronger!" said Chase.
"And bigger!" added Skye. "It could cover the entire Hidden Jungle soon!"

"I'm feeling the cold now, and so are the plants," replied Ryder.
"We need to find enough heat to keep them warm."
Then he had an idea!

"The volcano!" he said. "If we can send some superhot volcano gases over to the frozen lagoon, I can melt it and stop the storm!"
The pups used teamwork to dig an underground tunnel—and their plan worked!

"Now that the valley is unfrozen, I'm sure the big, big animals will be happy to stay down here," said Ryder.

Marshall even made a new friend—when he pulled a thorn out of the big tiger's paw!

Yay!